# The Monkey's Bargains
## and
## Other Folk-Tales

# The Monkey's Bargains
## and
## Other Folk-Tales

Collected by
**W. CROOKE**

Retold by
**W. H. D. ROUSE**

Illustrated by
**W. H. ROBINSON**

HAWK PRESS

Published by

**Hawk Press**
4836/24, Ansari Road, Daryaganj
New Delhi – 110 002
Phones : 9643330713, +91-11-23278618, +91-11-35676207
E-mail : thehawkpress@gmail.com
www.thehawkpress.com

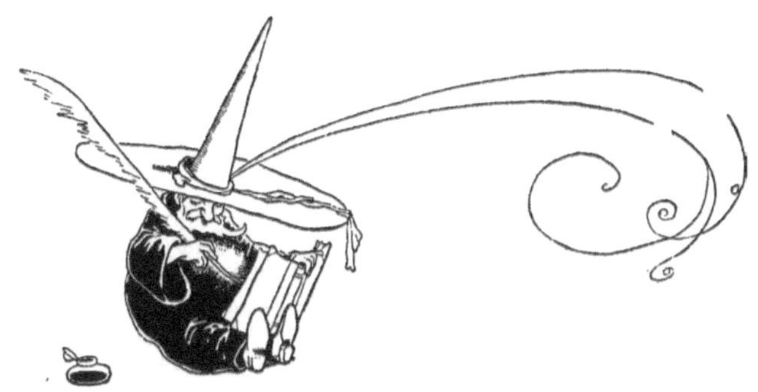

# Contents


| | |
|---|---|
| *Preface* | *vii* |
| A Crow is a Crow for ever | 1 |
| The Grateful Goat | 5 |
| The Cunning Jackal; or, the Biter Bit | 10 |
| The Farmer's Ass | 15 |
| The Parrot Judge | 20 |
| The Frog and the Snake | 24 |
| Little Miss Mouse and her Friends | 26 |
| The Jackal that Lost his Tail | 30 |
| The Wily Tortoise | 36 |
| The King of the Mice | 38 |
| The Valiant Blackbird | 44 |
| The Goat and the Hog | 50 |

The Parrot and the Parson 55
The Lion and the Hare 58
The Monkey's Bargains 60
The Monkey's Rebuke 69
The Bull and the Bullfinch 74

# Preface

THE stories contained in this little book are only a small part of a large collection of Indian folk-tales, made by Mr. Crooke in the course of the Ethnological Survey of the North-West Provinces and Oudh. Some were recorded by the collector from the lips of the jungle-folk of Mirzápur; others by his native assistant, Pandit Rámgharíb Chaubé. Besides these, a large number were reccived from all parts of the Provinces in response to a circular issued by Mr. J. C. Nesfield, the Director of Public Instruction, to all teachers of village schools.

The present selection is confined to the Beast Stories, which are particularly interesting as being mostly indigenous and little affected by so-called Aryan influence. Most of them are new, or have been published only in the *North Indian Notes and Queries*.

In the re-telling, for which Mr. Rouse is responsible, a number of changes have been made. The text of the book is meant for children, and consequently the first aim has been to make an interesting story. Those who study folk-tales for any scientific purpose will find all such changes marked in the Notes. If the change is considerable, the original document is summarised. It should be added that these documents are merely brief Notes in themselves, without literary interest. The Notes also give the source of each tale, and a few obvious parallels, or references to the literature of the subject.

# A Crow is a Crow for ever

There once was a very learned Bishop, who was very fond of bird's-nesting. One day he saw a fine large nest up in an elm-tree, and when he had climbed up he saw that it was full of young Crow-chicks. One of these chicks had such a winsome appearance, that the Bishop put him inside his hat, and took him home to the Palace.

In due time the Crow grew up, and as he heard around him continually the Bishop and his friends talking divinity, by degrees he became quite clever in divinity himself. He knew all the kings of Israel and Judah, and the cities of refuge, so that at last there was no question in a divinity paper he could not answer. Indeed, once when the examining Chaplain was ill, the Crow did his work for him.

The fame of this learned Crow spread far and wide, until at last it reached the King's ears. Now the Bishop had been expecting this all along, and ever since he found the young Crow he had been training him for a purpose. I am sorry to say he was rather a greedy man; and as he hoped to get something out of the King by the means of this Crow, he trained him to fly towards anything that shone bright, such as gold and silver.

"When the King asks me to show off my Crow," he thought,

"I will ask as a price anything the Crow may choose; and then doubtless he will fly to the King's crown, and I shall be King!"

At the first all fell out as he looked for. The King sent word to say he wanted to see the Crow. He was sitting in the garden, with his gold crown on, and all his courtiers around him; and then asked to hear him say all the kings of Israel and Judah.

"With pleasure, sire," said the Bishop; "if your Majesty will deign to grant him what he chooses for a reward. He has been well taught, and will not work for nothing."

"By all means," said the King; "let him choose his reward, and I will give it."

Then the Bishop took his Crow out of his hat, and the Crow said all the kings of Israel and Judah quite right, forwards and backwards, without a single mistake. The King was delighted: he could not have done as much.

"And now, sire," said the Bishop, "I will let him go, and tell him to choose his own prize."
So the Bishop let the Crow loose. The Crow was flying straight for the King's crown, when all on a sudden what should he spy but a dead cat! He turned off on the instant, and down he swooped on the dead cat. You know Crows eat dead things and offal; and this Crow liked a dead cat for dinner better than a gold crown.

The King laughed, the courtiers roared with merriment.
"Bishop," said the King, when he had done laughing, "your

Crow is easily pleased, it seems! Well, he has chosen his reward, and by my royal beard, he shall have it. Ha, ha, ha!"

But the Bishop felt very rueful indeed. All his pains and trouble lost, and nothing to show for it! He shook his head and went away, singing to himself a little chant he made up on the spot, all out of his own head--

> "I kept my Crow in a lovely cage,
> And taught him wisdom's holy page;
> But still 'tis true, whate'er he may know,
> A dirty Crow is a dirty Crow."

# The Grateful Goat

Once upon a time a Butcher bought a Goat; but as he was going to kill the Goat, and make him into meat for the table, the Goat opened his mouth, and said--

"If you kill me, Butcher, you will be a few shillings the richer; but if you spare my life, I will repay you for your kindness."

This Butcher had killed many goats in his day, but he never before heard one of them talk. Goats can talk to each other, as you must have heard; but most of them do not learn English. So the Butcher thought there must be something special about this Goat, and did not kill him.

The Goat felt very grateful that his life had been spared for a few more happy summers; and when he found himself free, the first thing he did was to go into the forest to see if he could find some means of repaying the Butcher's kind deed.

As he trotted along under the trees, stopping now and then to crop some tender shoot that came within reach, he met a Jackal.

"I am glad to see you, Goatee," said the Jackal; "and now I'm going to eat you."

"Don't be such a fool," said the Goat. "Can't you see I am nothing but skin and bones? Wait till I get fat. That's why I am here, just to get fat; and when I'm nice and fat, you may eat me and welcome."

The Goat was very skinny, in truth, and he pulled in his breath to make himself look more skinny. So the Jackal said--

"All right, look sharp, and be sure you look out for me on your way back."

"I shan't forget, Jackal," said the Goat. "Ta ta!"

By-and-by he fell in with a Wolf.

"Ha!" said the Wolf, smacking his lips; "here's what I want. Get ready, my Goat, for I am going to eat you."

"Oh, surely not," said the Goat; "a skinny old thing like me!" He drew in his breath again, and looked very skinny indeed. "I have come here to fatten myself, and when I'm fat, you shall eat me if you like."

"Well," said the Wolf, "you don't look like a prize Goat, I grant you. Go along then, but look out for me when you come back."

"Oh, I shall look out for you!" said the Goat, and away he trotted.

By-and-by he came to a church. He went into the church, and there he saw last Sunday's collection plate, full of gold coins. In that country, any one would have been ashamed to put coppers into the plate, not because they were rich, for they were not, but because they were generous. Now, Goats are not taught that they must not steal, but they think they have a right to whatever they can get hold of; so this Goat opened his mouth, and licked up all the sovereigns, and hid them under his tongue.

The Goat next went to a flower-shop, and asked the man who sold the flowers to make some wreaths, and cover him up with them, horns and all. So the man covered him up with flowers, till he looked like a large rose-bush. Then the Goat popped out a sovereign from his mouth, to pay the man, and very glad the man was to get so much for his roses.

Then the Goat set out on his homeward way. He looked out for the Wolf, as he had promised to do; and when the Wolf saw him coming along, he thought he was a rose-bush. The Wolf was not at all surprised to see a rose-bush walking along the road, for many were the strange things he had seen in his life; and if you come to think of it, this was no stranger than a Goat that could talk English.

"Good afternoon, Rose-bush," said the Wolf; "have you seen a Goat passing this way?"

"Oh yes," said the Goat, "I saw him a few minutes ago back there along the road."

"Many thanks, Rose-bush," said the Wolf; "I am much obliged to you," and away he ran in the direction in which the Goat had come.

By-and-by he came to the Jackal.

"Hullo, Rose-bush!" said the Jackal. "Have you seen a Goat anywhere as you came along?"

"Oh yes," replied the Goat, out of the roses; "I saw him just now, and he was talking to a big Wolf."

"Good heavens!" said the Jackal, "I must look sharp, if I want some Goat to-day," and off he galloped, in a great hurry.

In the evening he got to the Butcher's house.

"Hullo!" said the Butcher, "what have we here?" He knew that rose-bushes could not walk, but he could not make out what it was at all.

"Baa! baa!" said the Goat; "it's your grateful old Goat, come back to pay you for your kindness." And with these words, he spouted out all the sovereigns he found in the church, except the one he paid to the flower-man.

The Butcher was delighted to see so many sovereigns: he asked no questions, because he thought it wiser. He took the sovereigns, and found they were enough to keep him all his life, without killing any more goats. So he lived in peace, and the Goat spent his remaining years browsing comfortably in the Butcher's paddock.

# The Cunning Jackal

## Or, the Biter Bit

A Jackal upon a time a Butcher bought a Goat; but as he was going to kill the Goat, and make him into meat for the table, the Goat opened his mouth, and said--

lived on one side of a deep river, and on the other side were fields upon fields of ripe melons. The Jackal was always hungry, and he had eaten everything within reach; so he used to sit on the river bank and bemoan his luck. "All those ripe melons," said he, "and nobody to eat them but men. It is really a shame. I don't know what Providence is doing, to treat me so scurvily."

Perhaps Providence knew what it was about, and the Jackal, as you shall hear, deserved no better than he got.

As he sat one day by the river, moaning and groaning, a big Tortoise popped up his funny head out of the water. There was a big tear in each of the Tortoise's round eyes.

The Jackal stopped moaning and groaning when he saw the Tortoise. "What's the matter, Shelly?" said he. "Aren't you well?"

"Quite well, thank you," said the Tortoise, and the tears slowly rolled down his nose. He was going to call the Jackal Snarly, which was the nickname the Jackal went by; but he thought better of it, because it would have been rather rude. All the same, he did not like being called Shelly in that offhand way.

"Wife and brats all right?" asked the Jackal. "No measles or mumps?"

This was also very rude of the Jackal, because a Tortoise is sensitive about mumps. If he gets mumps when his head is inside his shell, he can't put it out; and if his head is outside, that is still worse, for it swells up so that he can't get it in again.

"No, thank you, my wife is all right," said the Tortoise, who was rather confused; "at least, she would be all right if I had one, but that's just it--I can't get a wife! Nobody will look at me! and that is my trouble," and two more big tears trickled down his nose.

At this moment an idea came into the Jackal's crafty head. "What a pity you didn't tell me before," said he; "I could easily have found you a wife last week, but now she has gone to live on the other side of the river."

"Do you really mean it?" said the Tortoise.

"Honour bright," answered the Jackal; "do I look like a person who would tell a lie?" He certainly did, only the Tortoise was too simple to see it.

The Tortoise rubbed away his tears on a stump, for he had no handkerchief, and brightened up considerably.

"I can carry you across, friend," said he, "if you will jump on my back."

The Jackal wanted nothing better, so down he jumped on the back of the Tortoise, and the Tortoise swam across. When they got across, the Tortoise was quite tired, because the Jackal was very heavy for a Tortoise to carry.

A fine time the Jackal had on the further side of the river. He ran about among the fields, and ate melons till he was nearly bursting. Every day the Tortoise came to the bank, asking whether the match was yet arranged, and every day the Jackal told him that all was going well. "You have no notion how pleased they are," said the Jackal. "Just see how fat I am getting. They feed me like a fighting-cock, all because of you." It was indeed because of the Tortoise that the Jackal was so well fed, but not as he meant it.

By-and-by the season of melons came to an end, and all that the Jackal had left were cut and sold in the market. Melons were dear that season, because the Jackal had eaten so many of them before they could be cut. Then the Jackal stole a white dress and a veil, and hung them on the stump of a tree which stood near the river side; and next day, when the Tortoise popped his funny head out of the water, said the Jackal--

"There's your wife at last, old Shelly! There she stands, dumb as a stone. Not a word will she have to say to you till I am out of the way, because she is too modest. Come, hurry up, Shell-fish, and take me across."

The Tortoise was angry at being called a shell-fish, because tortoises are not fish at all, and they feel insulted if you call them so. However, he was so glad to get a wife at last, that he said nothing, only presented his back for the Jackal to jump on. Flop! came the Jackal, so heavy by this time that it was all the Tortoise could do to get him across safely. If he was tired before, he was nearly dead now. But he swam across at last; and the Jackal ran off into the forest, chuckling at the simplicity of the poor Tortoise.

Back went our Tortoise across the river, and climbed up on the bank.

"Wife!" he called out, in a tender voice.
No answer.

Again he called "Wife!" but still no answer.

He could not make it out a bit. He crawled up to the stump which the Jackal had decked out in wedding finery, and put out his flapper to touch his wife's hand: lo and behold, it was only an old tree-stump.

The rage of the Tortoise knew no bounds, and he determined to have his revenge.

Next day the Jackal came down to drink at the river. The Tortoise was watching for him under water; and while the Jackal was drinking, the Tortoise nipped his teeth into the Jackal's leg.

How the Jackal did howl, to be sure! He was a great coward, and even used to cry when his teeth were pulled out by the dentist. So now he howled at the top of his voice, "Let me go! Let me go!"

But the Tortoise held on like grim death. He was too weak to pull the Jackal under, but he was too heavy for the Jackal to pull out; so there he bides his time. By-and-by the tide began to rise. The tide rose to the Jackal's middle, it rose to his head; and his last howlscame up from underneath the water in big bubbles, which showed that the crafty Jackal would play his mean tricks never more.

# The Farmer's Ass

There was once a Farmer, who had an Ass. It was the habit of this Ass to lift up his voice and bray, whenever he heard the church bells a-ringing. Now in the country where this Farmer lived, they used to believe that a man's soul passes when he dies into an animal, or something else. So this Farmer thought that any Ass that was fond of church bells, must have been a great saint in some former life. Accordingly, he named his Ass St. Anthony.

All his life long, this Ass served the Farmer faithfully, and earned him a great deal of money. At last the Ass died of old age.

The Farmer was very sad and sorry when his Ass died. "My Ass served me faithfully," said he, "and it's only fair he should have a good funeral." So he sent for the undertaker, and told him to make a big coffin, and put it on a hearse, and buried the Ass with great splendour.

Then he shaved off every scrap of hair from his head, as the custom was in those parts when anybody died, and gave a funeral feast to all his relations, and dressed himself in black.

Next time he went to the Grocer's to buy sugar, the Grocer noticed his head shaved bare, and the black clothes, so he knew some one must be dead, a relation or a great friend.

"I am sorry to see you have lost some one," said he; "who is it?"

"St. Anthony is dead," said the Farmer.

"Dear me," said the Grocer, "and I never heard of it. How very sad!" Thought he to himself, "I had best have my head shaved too, or else people will call me hard-hearted."

So when the Farmer had bought his sugar, and was gone, the Grocer went to the Barber and had his head shaved. Then he put on a black coat and necktie.

By-and-by a Soldier came to have a chat with his friend the Grocer.

"Ods bobs!" said he, "what's the matter, man?"

"St. Anthony is dead," said the Grocer solemnly, and wiped away a tear.

"You don't say so," said the Soldier. Off he went straight to the Barber, and made him shave his head; then he bought a piece of crape to tie round his left arm.

He told the news to all the men of his regiment, and they all felt so much sympathy with this soldier that they shaved their heads too.

Next day on parade, there was the whole regiment shaved to a man.

"What's the meaning of this?" asked the General.

The Sergeant saluted, and told him that St. Anthony was dead.

"Is he? By Jove," said the General, "then I dismiss this parade," and off he galloped on his war-horse to the nearest Barber, who shaved his head like the men's. On the way back, he saw the Prime Minister going to Court. "May I ask," said the Prime Minister suavely, "to what untoward circumstance is due the erasure of your capillary covering?"

"St. Anthony is dead," answered the General.

"Dear, dear," said the Prime Minister, "you don't say so. He was doubtless an ornament to the party, and it is meet that I should testify my respect." Then the Prime Minister too went off to get his head shaved, and appeared before the King without a single hair.

"What's the matter?" asked the King; "anybody dead, hey, hey, hey?"

"If it please your Majesty," said the Prime Minister, "St. Anthony is dead."

"What a loss for our kingdom," said the King; "what a loss! what a loss! Excuse me a moment," and away he went to get his head shaved.

When the Queen saw him, she wanted to know why his head was shaved.

"St. Anthony is dead," answered the King.

"And who is St. Anthony?" asked the Queen.

"I don't know who he is," said the King, "a friend of the Prime Minister's."

So the Prime Minister was asked who St. Anthony was; and replied that he did not himself know him, but the General spoke of him in the highest terms. The General said that St. Anthony was not a personal friend, but he was well known in the regiment. After inquiry amongst the men, it was found that only one of them could tell anything about St. Anthony, and all he knew was that his friend the Grocer shaved his head in memory of him. The Grocer referred them to the Farmer, and the Farmer was out inthe fields.

Then the King sent a messenger on horseback to find the Farmer and bring him to court. The Farmer was brought into court, and when he saw the King and the Prime Minister and General all in mourning, he was very much surprised. The King said to him, "Farmer, who is St. Anthony?"

"If it please your Majesty, he was my Ass."

The King, and the Prime Minister, and the General felt very foolish to have gone into mourning for an Ass. They put off their black clothes, but it was not so easy to get their hair back again; and so for a month or two the King, and the Prime Minister, and the General, and all the regiment of Body Guards, went about in wigs.

# The Parrot Judge

'Twas once a Fowler who caught a young Parrot. He kept the Parrot in his house, hoping that it would pick up something to say, but the Parrot learnt nothing at all. Then he set to work at teaching it; but after six months the Parrot had only learnt to say two things: one was "Of course," and the other was "Certainly."

Seeing that his trouble was wasted, the Fowler took him to market in a gilt cage, in order to catch the eye of customers. He cried in a loud voice, "Who'll buy! who'll buy! here's a Parrot which can say anything in the world! Here's a clever Parrot who knows what he is talking about! If you want a question answered here's the Parrot to answer you, no matter what it may be! Who'll buy, who'll buy?" Everybody crowded round to see the wonderful Parrot.

The King happened to be passing by, and heard all this to-do about a Parrot. Said he to the Fowler--

"Is it really true about your Parrot?"
"Ask him, sire," said the Fowler.

"Parrot," said the King, "do you know English?"

"Of course," said the Parrot, in a tone of scorn, turning up his beak; as who should say, "What a question to ask *me*."

"Can you decide knotty points of law?" the King went on.

"Certainly," said the Parrot, with great confidence.

"This is the bird for me," said the King, and asked his price. The price was a thousand pounds. The King paid a thousand pounds to the Fowler, and departed.

A big price, you will say, for a Parrot. So it was; but the King had a reason for paying it. The Judge of the City had just died, and the King could not find another. Hundreds of men offered to do the work. Some wanted too much money, more than the King could pay; some were reasonable, but knew no law; and the cheaper ones who professed to know everything were all Germans, whom the King would not have at any price. When he heard of this wise Parrot, thought he, "Here's my Judge; he will want no wages but sugar and chickweed, and he will take no bribes."

So the Parrot was made Judge, and sat on a big throne, with a white wig and a red robe lined with ermine.

Next day, the Parrot was in Court, and a case came up for judgment. It was a murder case, and when the evidence had been heard, the pleader on the murderer's side finished up his speech by saying, "And now, my Lord, you must admit that my client is innocent."

Said the Parrot, "Of course."

Everybody thought this rather odd, because the other side had not yet been heard; and, besides, the man was caught in the act. However, they held their tongues and waited.

Then the prosecutor got up, and made a long speech, at the end of which he said, "It is no longer possible to doubt that the prisoner at the bar is guilty. Two witnesses saw him do the deed, and half-a-dozen caught him just as he was pulling the knife out of the body. I therefore call upon you, my Lord, to pass sentence of death."

Said the Parrot, "Certainly."

At this the King pricked up his ears. The man could not be innocent of course, and yet certainly guilty, at the same time. So he turned to the Judge and said--

"If you go against evidence so clear, Judge, I shall begin to suspect that you killed the man yourself."

Said the Parrot, "Certainly."

You may imagine the hubbub that arose in Court when the Judge said this! Everybody saw that the King had made a mistake in his Judge, and even the King himself began to suspect that something was wrong. So he said,
rather angrily, to the Parrot--

"Then it is your head ought to be chopped off."

Said the Parrot, "Of course."

"Chop off his head, then," cried the King; and they took away the Parrot and chopped off his head without delay; and all the while he was being dragged along, he called out, "Certainly," "Certainly," "Certainly."

# The Frog and the Snake

A FROG and a Snake had a quarrel as to which could give the more deadly bite. They agreed to try it on the next opportunity.

A Man came to bathe in the pond where these two creatures lived. The Snake bit him under the water, while the Frog floated on the top. "Something has bitten me!" the Man called out to his friends.

"What is it?" they asked.

Then he saw the Frog swimming on the top of the water. "Oh, it's only a Frog," said he. Then he went away, and no harm came of it.

The next time that Man came to bathe in the pond, the Frog bit him under the water, while the Snake swam on the top.

"Oh dear!" said the Man, "a Snake has bitten me!" The Man died.
"Now," said the Frog, "you will admit that my bite is more poisonous than yours."

"I deny it altogether," said the Snake.

So they agreed to refer their dispute to the King of the Snakes. The Snake King listened to their arguments, and decided in favour of the Snake, and said the Man had died of fright.

"Of course," grumbled the Frog, "the Snake King sides with the Snake."

So both of them bit the Frog, and he died, and that was the end of him.

# Little Miss Mouse and her Friends

There and a Snake had a quarrel as to which could give the more deadly bite. They agreed to try it on the next opportunity.

was once a little Lady-Mouse that lived in a field. She was all alone in the world, a little old maid, and she very much wanted a friend. But every creature turned up his nose at the poor little Mouse, and not a friend could she get; until at last a Clod of earth took pity upon her. Then the Mouse and the Clod became firm friends, and went about everywhere together. The Mouse walked upon her four legs, and the Clod rolled along like a cricket ball.

One day the Mouse wanted a bathe; and nothing would serve, but the Clod must go bathe along with her. In vain the Clod protested that she did not like water; that she had never washed in her life; that she could not swim: Miss Mousie would take no denial, and said severely, that if the Clod had never washed before, it was high time to begin. So at length the Clod was persuaded, and into the river they went. Mousie went in first, and the Clod rolled in afterwards; but no sooner had the poor Clod rolled into the river, than what was Miss Mousie's horror to see her melt away in the water, and disappear.

Mousie was now friendless again, and loudly complained to the River that he had stolen away her favourite Clod.

"I am very sorry," the River said; "I really couldn't help melting a thing so soft. I can't give you back your Clod, but I will give you a Fish instead."

This comforted Mousie, and she took her Fish and went home. Then she put the Fish on the top of a post, to dry. Down swooped a big Kite, and flew away with the Fish.

"O my poor Fish," wailed Miss Mousie, "to be taken away before we had a word together." Then she went to the Post, and demanded her Fish back again. "I gave him to you," said Mousie, "and you are responsible for
him."

Said the Post, "I am very sorry that I cannot give you back your Fish, but I will give you some Wood."

Mousie was grateful for this kindness on the part of the Post. So she took a piece of Wood in exchange for the Fish.

Mousie and the Wood went off to buy some sweets at the Confectioner's. While Mousie was eating the sweets, the Confectioner's wife burnt the Wood in the fire.

Mousie finished the sweets, and when she turned round to look for her Wood, lo and behold it was gone. With tears in her eyes she begged the Confectioner's wife to give her back the Wood, but the Confectioner's wife said--

"I am very sorry I cannot give you back the Wood, because it is burnt; but I will give you some Cakes instead."

This made Miss Mousie happy again, and she took the Cakes. Then she paid a visit to the Shepherd's pen; and while she was talking to the Shepherd, a Goat ate up her cakes.

"Give me back my Cakes, Mr. Shepherd," said Mousie, not seeing the Cakes anywhere.

"I'm very sorry I can't do that," answered the Shepherd, "because I am afraid one of my goats has eaten them; but if you like, you may have a Kid instead."

This was better and better. Mousie was charmed with her Kid and led it off to the music-shop, where she had to pay a bill. While the man was writing a receipt to the bill, his wife killed the Kid, and began to roast it for dinner. Mousie looked round, and wanted to know where her Kid was?

"I rather think," said the Music-man, "that the nice odour of roast meat which tickles your nostrils, comes from that Kid. I'm sorry I can't give you the Kid back, but you may have the best drum in my shop."

Mousie did not like the Drum so well as her Kid; but needs must, and she picked out a drum, and went away with it on her shoulder. By-and-by she came to a place where women were beating rice, to get the grains away from the husk. She hung up her Drum on a peg, while she watched the women husking the rice. Bang! flap! a woman drove her pestle right through the Drum.

Poor Mousie. It seemed as if her misfortunes would never end. When she asked the woman for her Drum again, there it was, burst. The tears ran down her cheeks.

"We are very sorry," the women all said, "that we cannot give you back your Drum; but you can have a Girl instead, if you like."

This brought smiles to Miss Mousie's sad face, and she dried her tears. The women gave her a nice Girl, and Mousie took the Girl home. They set up house together, and planted a crop of corn. The corn ripened, and they went out to cut it. Miss Mouse was a wee mousie, and was quite hidden among the stalks of the corn. While the Girl was cutting the corn with a sickle, she did not see poor little Mousie, so she cut her in two, and that was the end of her.

# The Jackal that Lost his Tail

There was once a Farmer, who used to go out every morning to work in his field, and his wife used to bring him dinner at noon. One day, as the Farmer's wife was carrying out the dinner to the field, she met a Jackal, who said--

"Where are you going?"
Said she, "To my husband, and this is his dinner."
Said the Jackal, "Give me some, or I will bite you."
So the woman had to give the Jackal some of this food. And when her husband saw it, he said--

"What a small dinner you have brought me to-day!"

"A Jackal met me," replied his wife, "and threatened to bite me if I gave him none."

"All right," said the Farmer, "to-morrow I'll settle with that Jackal."

On the morrow, the Farmer's wife went after the plough, and the Farmer dressed up in her clothes and carried out the dinner. Again the Jackal appeared.

"Give me some of that," said he, "or I'll bite you."

"Yes, yes, good Mr. Jackal," said the man, "you shall have some, only don't bite me."

Then he set down the plate and the Jackal began to eat.

"Just scratch my back, you, woman," said the Jackal, "while I am eating my dinner."

"Yes, sir; yes, sir," said the man. He began gently to tickle and scratch the back of the Jackal, and in the middle, suddenly out with his knife, and slish! cut off the Jackal's tail.

The Jackal jumped up and capered about. "Yow-ow-ow!" he went, "what has come to my tail? Oh dear! how shall I swish away the flies? Oh dear, how it hurts! Yow-ow-ow!" Away he scuttled, as fast as his legs could carry him.

When he got home, all the Jackals came round him, and asked what had become of his tail. The Jackal was ashamed to have lost his tail, which was a particularly long and fine tail; but he pretended to like it.

"Poor fellow!" said the Jackals, "where is your tail?"

"I had it cut off," said the Jackal, "and good riddance. It was always in my way. Why, I never could sit down in comfort, and now look here!" He sat down on the place where his tail used to be, and looked proudly round. "Now, you try!" said he.

They all tried, and found that their tails got underneath them when they sat, and it hurt their tails rather.

"We never thought of that before," said they; "we must get rid of these things. Who cut off yours?"

"A kind Farmer's wife," said the first Jackal. Then he told them where the Farmer's wife lived.

That evening, a knock came at the Farmer's door, as the Farmer and his wife were sitting at tea.

"Come in!" said the Farmer.

The door opened, and in trooped a number of Jackals. "Please, Mr. Farmer," said they, "we want you kindly to cut off our tails."

"Willingly," said the Farmer; whipt out his knife, and in a jiffy slish! slish! slish! off came the Jackals' tails.

"Yow-ow-ow!" went the Jackals, capering about, "we didn't think it would hurt!" Away they went, and all the woods echoed that night with yowling and howling.

When they all got home, they found the first Jackal waiting for them. He laughed in their faces. "Now we're all alike," said he, "all in the same boat."

"Are we?" said the other Jackals, and set on him and tore him to pieces.
"Now we must have our revenge on the Farmer," said the Jackals when they had eaten up their friend. So next morning they scampered off to the Farmer's house.

The Farmer was out, and his wife was gathering fuel.

"Good morning, Mrs. Farmer," said the Jackals; "we have come to eat the Farmer for cutting our tails off."

"Ah, poor fellow," said the Farmer's wife, "he is dead. When he saw how it hurt you to have your tails cut off, he just lay down on the bed, and died of grief."

"That's unlucky," said the Jackals.

"But we are preparing the funeral feast," she went on, "you see I am now getting fuel for it. Will you give us the pleasure of your company to dinner?"

"Gladly," said the Jackals; "we should like to see the last of the poor fellow;" then they ran away.

At dinner-time, they all came back, and found chairs put for them, and plates round the table, with the woman at one end.

"You can sit like Christians now," said the Farmer's wife, "so I have set you a chair apiece."

"Thanks," said the Jackals; "that is thoughtful."

"But I know," the Farmer's wife went on, "what quarrelsome creatures you are over your meat. Don't you think I had better tie you to your chairs, and then each will have to keep to his own plateful?"

"A good plan," the Jackals said, wagging their heads. They had now no tails to wag, and they had to wag something. So the Farmer's wife tied them tight to their chairs.

"But how shall we eat?" said the Jackals, who could not stir a paw.

"Oh, no fear for that, I'll feed you."

Then she brought out a steaming mess, and put it in the middle of the table. All the Jackals sniffed at the steam, and all their eyes were fixed greedily upon the meat. They began to struggle.

"Softly, softly, good Jackals!" said the Farmer's wife.

But what a surprise awaited the Jackals! They were so intent upon watching the Farmer's wife and the meat, that none of them heard the door open, and none of them saw the Farmer himself creep softly in, with a great club in his hand. The first news they had of it was crack! crack! crack!

All but three of the Jackals looked round, and they saw these three of their comrades with their heads smashed in, lolling back in the chairs. The Farmer held the club poised in the air; down it came crack! on the head of the fourth Jackal. Then all the others began yowling and struggling to get free; but in vain, the cords held them fast, they could not stir; and in five minutes all the Jackals lay dead on the floor.

After that the Farmer ploughed in peace, and no one molested the Farmer's wife when she brought his dinner.

# The Wily Tortoise

*A* Flower was bird-catching in the jungle, and snared a wild goose. As he was carrying home his goose, he sat down by a pond. In this pond lived a Tortoise, and the Tortoise put up his nose out of the pond to sniff the air. He saw the Fowler and the Goose, and being a very innocent Tortoise, he feared no harm, but began to waddle towards them.

"Take care, friend!" said the Goose. "This Fowler has caught me, and he will catch you!"

The Tortoise waddled into the water again. "Many thanks, friend," said he. "One good turn deserves another." So saying, he dived down into the pond, and brought up a ruby.

"Here, Mr. Fowler," said he, "take this ruby, and let my friend the Goose go."
The Fowler took the ruby, but he was very greedy, so he said-- "If you will bring me a pair to this, I will let the Goose go."

The Tortoise dived down, and brought up another ruby. Then the Fowler let go the Goose, and said to the Tortoise, "Now hand over that ruby."

The Tortoise said, "Forgive me, I have made a mistake, and brought up the wrong ruby. Let me see the first, and if it does not match, I will try again." The Fowler gave back the first ruby. "As I thought," said the Tortoise. Down he dived into the pond. The Fowler waited a good long time, but nothing was seen of the Tortoise. As you have guessed, when the Tortoise found himself safe at the bottom of the pond, he stayed there. The Fowler tore his hair, and went home, wishing he had not been so greedy.

# The King of the Mice

Far away in the forest was the Kingdom of Mouseland. There was a great city, where every Mouse had his little house, with doors and windows, tables and chairs, books for the grown-up Mice, and toys for the children; there were little shops, where the Mice bought clothes and food, and everything they wanted; there was a little church where they went on Sunday, and a reverend little Mouse in a little lawn surplice to preach to them; there was a little palace, and in this palace lived the little Mouse King.

Now it happened that a caravan passed through the Kingdom of the Mice. Not that the men of the caravan knew what a wonderful kingdom they were in. They thought it was just like any other part of the forest, and if they did happen to pass a Mouse fortress, or farmyard, they thought them nothing but heaps of earth. Just so if you were to fly up in a balloon, and look down on your own house from the air, it would seem like a little doll's-house, not fit for a child to live in. This caravan, as I have said, was passing through Mouseland, and encamped in part of it once to spend the night. One of the Camels was very sick, and as the owner of the Camel thought it was sure to die, he left it behind when the caravan went away.

But the Camel did not die; he very soon got as well as ever he was. And when he got well he also got hungry; so he strode all over Mouseland, eating up the crops of the Mice, and treading their houses down, until at last he came to the Mouse King's park. He ate a great many trees in the Mouse King's park, and the Keeper went in a hurry and flurry to tell the King.

"O King," said he, "a mountain several miles high has walked into your park, and is eating everything up."

"We must make an example of this mountain," said the King, "or the whole earth may be moving next. Sandy," said he to his Prime Minister, who was a Fox, "go and fetch that mountain to me."

So Sandy the Prime Minister went to seek the mountain that was eating the King's park. Next morning, back he came, leading the Camel by his nose-string.

When the Camel saw how little the King of the Mice seemed to be, he began to grunt and gurgle, and sniffed with his funny mouth. You know a Camel has a mouth which looks as though it had two slits in it, of the shape of a cross; and when he wants to show his contempt for anything he pokes out his mouth like a four-leaved clover, and makes you feel very small. "Hullo," said the Camel, "is this your King? I thought it was the Lion who sent for me. I would never have come for a speck like this." Then he turned round, and walked out of court, and began to eat everything he came across.

The King was very angry, but what could he do? He had to swallow the insult, and make the best of it. However, he determined to watch his chance of revenge; and soon he got it. For after a few days, the Camel's nose-string became entangled in a creeper, and he could not get away, do what he would. Then Sandy the Fox came by, and saw him in this plight. Imagine his joy to see his enemy at his mercy! Off he ran, and soon brought the King to that place. Then the King said--

"O Camel, you despised my words, and see the result. Your sin has found you out."

"O mighty King," said the Camel, quite humble now, "indeed I confess my fault, and I pray you to forgive me. If you will only save me, I will be your faithful servant."

The Mouse King was not of a spiteful nature, and as soon as he heard the Camel ask forgiveness his heart grew soft. He climbed up the creeper, and gnawed through the Camel's nose-string, and set the Camel free.

The Camel, I am glad to say, kept his word; and he became a servant of the Mouse King. He was so big and strong that he could carry loads which would have needed thousands of Mice to carry; and by his help the King made very strong walls and forts around his city, so that he had no fear of enemies. When there was nothing else to do, the Camel even blacked the Mouse King's boots, rather than be idle.

So things went on for a long time. But one day some Woodcutters came into the forest. These men lived all together in a village of their own, and they used to build houses of wood. When anybody wanted a house, he told the Woodcutters, and they used to leave their village and go into the woods. Then they cut down the trees, and sawed them into planks, and shaped them into the parts of a house. When the house was finished, they put numbers on all the parts, and took it to pieces again, and put it on a raft; and the raft floated down the great river to the place where the house had been ordered. Then they put up the house in a very short time, because you see it was all ready made, and only had to be put together.

These Woodcutters, then, came and settled for a while near the borders of Mouseland; and in the course of their wanderings they found the stray Camel. They promptly seized him, and carried him off.

When Sandy told the King what had happened, the Mouse King was very angry indeed. He sent a detachment of his bodyguard, armed cap-à-pie, to fetch the Woodcutters into his presence. The bodyguard captured two of them, and led them back bound. Then the King demanded his Camel.

"Pooh, silly little Mouse," said the Woodcutters. "If you want it, you must fetch it."

"I will," said the King of the Mice. "Tell your chief, whoever he is, that I hereby declare war upon him."

The Woodcutters laughed, and went away.

Then the Mouse King gathered together all his subjects, millions and millions of sturdy Mice; and they set out for the village of the Woodcutters. The Woodcutters had by this time finished their job, and they had been paid a good round sum of money for it; and the money was carefully put away, with all the other money they had, in a treasury.

Now the Mice were not able to meet big Woodcutters in the field, but they had their own tactics. Night and day they burrowed under the earth. First they made for the treasury; and though the treasury had stone walls, they got up easily through the floor, where no danger was expected, and one by one they carried off every coin from the treasury, until it was as bare as the palm of your hand. Then they got underneath all the houses of the village; and thousands and millions of Mice were
busy all day and all night in carrying out little baskets of earth from beneath the foundations. Thus it happened, that very soon the Woodcutters' village was standing on a thin shell of earth, and underneath it was a great hole.

Now was the time to strike the blow. The layer of earth was so thin, that the least shock would destroy it. So the Mouse King wrote a letter to the Woodcutter Chief, asking once more for his Camel, and in the letter he hid a little packet of snuff. He put the letter in the post, and waited.

Next day, as the Woodcutter Chief was sitting in his house, the postman came to the door--Rat-tat. The footman brought in a letter, and the Woodcutter Chief opened it. He read it through, and laughed. Then he waved it in the air, and said, "Let them come." As he waved the letter in the air, all the snuff fell out of it upon his nose. The Woodcutter gave a terrific sneeze, Tishoo! Tishoo! The thin shell of earth could not stand the shock; it trembled, and crumbled, and fell in, and all the Woodcutters fell in too, and all their village, and nothing was left of them but a big hole.

Then the Mouse King and his army went back to Mouseland; and though they never got the old Camel back (for he was swallowed up along with the Woodcutters), yet no one ever molested Mouseland again.

# The Valiant Blackbird

A Blackbird and his mate lived together on a tree. The Blackbird used to sing very sweetly, and one day the King heard him in passing by, and sent a Fowler to catch him. But the Fowler made a mistake; he did not catch Mr. Blackbird, who sang so sweetly, but Mrs. Blackbird, who could hardly sing at all. However, he did not know the difference, to look at her, nor did the King when he got the bird; but a cage was made for Mrs. Blackbird, and there she was kept imprisoned.

When Mr. Blackbird heard that his dear spouse was stolen, he was very angry indeed. He determined to get her back, by hook or by crook. So he got a long sharp thorn, and tied it at his waist by a thread; and on his head he put the half of a walnut-shell for a helmet, and the skin of a dead frog served for body-armour. Then he made a little kettle-drum out of the other half of the walnut-shell; and he beat his drum, and proclaimed war upon the King.

As he walked along the road, beating his drum, he met a Cat.

"Whither away, Mr. Blackbird?" said the Cat.

"To fight against the King," said Mr. Blackbird.

"All right," said the Cat, "I'll come with you: he drowned my kitten."

"Jump into my ear, then," says Mr. Blackbird. The Cat jumped into the Blackbird's ear, and curled up, and went to sleep: and the Blackbird marched along, beating his drum.

Some way further on, he met some Ants.

"Whither away, Mr. Blackbird?" said the Ants.

"To fight against the King," said Mr. Blackbird.

"All right," said the Ants, "we'll come too; he poured hot water down our hole."

"Jump into my ear," said Mr. Blackbird. In they jumped, and away went Blackbird, beating upon his drum.

Next he met a Rope and a Club. They asked him, whither away? and when they heard that he was going to fight against the King, they jumped into his ear also, and away he went.

Not far from the King's palace, Blackbird had to cross over a River. "Whither away, friend Blackbird?" asked the River. Quoth the Blackbird, "To fight against the King."

"Then I'll come with you," said the River.

"Jump into my ear," says the Blackbird. Blackbird's ears were pretty full by this time, but he found room somewhere for the River, and away he went.

Blackbird marched along until he came to the palace of the King. He knocked at the door, thump, thump.

"Who's there?" said the Porter.

"General Blackbird, come to make war upon the King, and get back his wife."

The Porter laughed so at the sight of General Blackbird, with his thorn, and his frogskin, and his drum, that he nearly fell off his chair. Then he escorted Blackbird into the King's presence.

"What do you want?" said the King.

"I want my wife," said the Blackbird, beating upon his drum, rub-a-dub-dub, rub-a-dub-dub.

"You shan't have her," said the King.

"Then," said the Blackbird, "you must take the consequences." Rub-a-dub-dub went the drum.

"Seize this insolent bird," said the King, "and shut him up in the henhouse. I don't think there will be much left of him in the morning."

The servants shut up Blackbird in the henhouse. When all the world was asleep, Blackbird said--

"Come out, Pussy, from my ear,
There are fowls in plenty here;
Scratch them, make their feathers fly,
Wring their necks until they die."

Out came Pussy-cat in an instant. What a confusion there was in the henhouse. Cluck-cluck-cluck went the hens, flying all over the place; but no use: Pussy got them all, and scratched out their feathers, and wrung their necks. Then she went back into Blackbird's ear, and Blackbird went to sleep.

When morning came, the King said to his men, "Go, fetch the carcass of that insolent bird, and give the Chickens an extra bushel of corn." But when they entered the henhouse, Blackbird was singing away merrily on the roost, and all the fowls lay around in heaps with their necks wrung.

They told the King, and an angry King was he. "To-night," said he, "you must shut up Blackbird in the stable." So Blackbird was shut up in the stable, among the wild Horses.

At midnight, when all the world was asleep, Blackbird said--

"Come out, Rope, and come out, Stick,
Tie the Horses lest they kick;
Beat the Horses on the head,
Beat them till they fall down dead."

Out came Club and Rope from Blackbird's ear; the Rope tied the horses, and the Club beat them, till they died. Then the Rope and the Club went back into the Blackbird's ear, and Blackbird went to sleep.

Next morning the King said--
"No doubt my wild Horses have settled the business of that Blackbird once for all. Just go and fetch out his corpse."

The servants went to the wild Horses' stable. There was Blackbird, sitting on the manger, and drumming away on his walnut-shell; and all round lay the dead bodies of the Horses, beaten to death.

If the King was angry before, he was furious now. His horses had cost a great deal of money; and to be tricked by a Blackbird is a poor joke.

"All right," said the King, "I'll make sure work of it to-night. He shall be put with the Elephants."

When night came the Blackbird was shut up in the Elephants' shed. No sooner was all the world quiet, than Blackbird began to sing--

"Come from out my ear, you Ants,
Come and sting the Elephants;
Sting their trunk, and sting their head,
Sting them till they fall down dead."

Out came a swarm of Ants from the Blackbird's ear. They crawled up inside the Elephants' trunks, they burrowed into the Elephants' brains, and stung them so sharply that the Elephants all went mad, and died.

Next morning, as before, the King sent for the Blackbird's carcass; and, instead of finding his carcass, the servants found the Blackbird rub-a-dub-dubbing on his drum, and the dead Elephants piled all round him.

This time the King was fairly desperate. "I can't think how he does it," said he, "but I must find out. Tie him to-night to my bed, and we'll see."

So that night Blackbird was tied to the King's bed. In the middle of the night, the King (who had purposely kept awake) heard him sing--

"Come out, River, from my ear,
Flow about the bedroom here;
Pour yourself upon the bed,
Drown the King till he is dead."

Out came the River, pour-pour-pouring out of the Blackbird's ear. It flooded the room, it floated the King's bed, the King began to get wet.

"In Heaven's name, General Blackbird," said the King, "take your wife, and begone."

So Blackbird received his wife again, and they lived happily ever after.

# The Goat and the Hog

A Goat  and a Hog were great friends, and for a long time they lived together. But they were poor, and one day the Goat said to the Hog--

"Good-bye, friend Hog! I am going to seek my fortune."

"Ugh! ugh! ugh!" said the Hog. It was kindly meant, for that was all the ignorant Hog could say. He intended to bid good-bye to his friend, and to wish him good luck.

The Goat trotted along till he came to the nearest town. He found a grain-shop with nobody in it; so in went our Goat, and ate his fill of the Grain, and whatever he could find. Then he went into the inner room, and sat down.

By-and-by the shopman came in; his little girl was with him, and the little girl began to cry for sugar.

"Go and get some out of the cupboard," said the shopman.

The little girl ran into the inner room to get the sugar, but the Goat was there. And when the Goat saw the little girl, he cried out, in a solemn and loud voice--

> "Little girl, go run, go run,
> Or your life is nearly done!
> And my crumpled horns I'll stick
> Through your little body quick!"

The little girl ran out shrieking. "What is it, my dear?" said her father.

"A demon, father!" she said; "save me from his crumpled horn."

What a terrible thing to happen in a quiet household! The poor man did not know what to do. So he sent for all his relations, and they advised him to try what the parson could do.

So the Parson was sent for, and the Clerk, and the Sexton, with bell, book, and candle. They lit the candle, and opened the book (I think it was a Latin Grammar, which they judged would be enough to scare any demon), and rang the bell; and then the Parson, with his heart in his boots, advanced into the room.

Instantly a horrid groan burst upon his ears (or so he thought), and a deep voice said--

"Parson, fly! or I will poke
This my crumpled horn into you!
You'll admit it is no joke
When you feel its point go through you!
Sexton, dig his grave, and then
Let the Clerk reply, Amen!"

The Parson dropt his Latin Grammar, and ran away, nor did he stop until he was safe in his own church.

At this the Shopman went down on his knees, and put his hands together, and said--

"O most respectable Demon! whoever you are, I pray you do me no harm; and I will worship you, and offer you anything you may desire."
Then the Goat came majestically out, walking upon his hind legs, with his grey beard flowing from his chin, and he said--

"Put wreaths and jewels about my neck, and on each of my

horns, and round my paws and my tail, and give me sweetmeats to eat, and I will do you no harm."

The Shopman made haste to do all this; he wreathed the Goat with flowers, and put all his wife's jewels upon the horns and paws, and all the jewels he could borrow from his neighbours.

The Goat went home, and showed all this magnificence to his friend the Hog. The Hog winked his greedy little eyes, and somehow made his friend understand that he would like some too. Then the Goat told him how he got the things, and showed him the way to the place.

So the Hog went to the same shop, and found it empty. The Shopman and his little girl had gone out to tell all the town what adventures they had passed through. The Hog grubbed up all he could find to eat, and then went and sat in the inner room.

Soon the Shopman and his little girl came back. The little girl ran inside to take off her little hat, and what does she see but a big black Hog sitting there! The Hog remembered his lesson, and wanted to say some terrible thing as the Goat had done; but all he could get out was--

"Ugh! ugh! ugh!"
This did not frighten the little girl at all. She ran out to her father, saying--

"O papa! there is a big black Hog inside!"
The Shopman got out his knife, and whetted it on the grindstone, and then he went into the room.

"Ugh! ugh! ugh!" said the Hog.

The Shopman said nothing, but stuck his knife into the Hog. Then there was a squealing and squalling, if you like! But in two minutes the Hog was dead, and in two hours he was skinned and cut up, and by nightfall, the Shopman and his little girl, and all their friends, were sitting round a delicious leg of roast pork, and the Sexton rang the bell for dinner, and the Parson said grace, and the Clerk said Amen.

# The Parrot and the Parson

There was once a Banker who taught his Parrot the speech of men. The Parrot made such progress that he was soon able to take part in any conversation, and he astonished every one by his intelligence.

One day a Parson came by the Parrot.

"My respects to your Reverence," said the Parrot.

The Parson looked all round him, he looked down at his feet, he looked up into the sky; but no one could he see who might have spoken to him. He could not make it out; he thought it must have been a ghost. Then the Parrot spoke again. "It was I who saluted you," said he. The Parrot was close to the Parson's ear, and now at length the Parson saw him. The Parrot went on--

"O reverend Sir, you teach men how to get free from the chains of their sins. May it please you to tell me how to escape from this cage?"

This was a practical question, but the Parson's advice was not usually asked on such points. He did not know what to say.

"I fear I can be of no use to you," said he, "but I will consult my Solicitor."

The Parson went to see his Solicitor, and paid him six and eightpence. He might have bought the Parrot, cage and all, for half that; but, as I said, he was not a practical man. When he told the Solicitor what business he came about, the Solicitor said nothing at all, but fell down in a faint.

"What can I have said to make him faint?" the Parson thought. "Perhaps it is the hot weather." He poured water over the Solicitor's face, and by-and-by the Solicitor came to.

The Parson was much distressed at having thrown away six and eightpence; but he knew it would be of no use asking the Solicitor to give any of it back, so he did not try. He went back to the Parrot and said--

"Dearly beloved bird, I much regret having no information to give you which may be of use. The fact is, no sooner did I put your question to my worthy Solicitor, than he fell down in a dead faint."

"Oh," said the Parrot, "many thanks, Parson."

The Parson went away to the parish meeting. When he had gone, the Parrot stretched himself out on the bottom of his cage, and shut his eyes, and cocked up his feet in the air.

By-and-by the Banker came in, and saw his Parrot lying on his back, with his feet pointing to the sky.

"Poor Poll," said he, "you're dead, my pretty Poll."

He opened the door of the cage, and took out the bird, and laid him on the ground. Immediately the Parrot opened his wings and flew away.

# The Lion and the Hare

Once upon a time there was a Lion, who used daily to devour one of the beasts of the forest. They had to come up one after another, when called for. At last it came to the Hare's turn to be eaten, and he did not want to be eaten at all. He lingered and he dallied, and when at last he plucked up courage to come, he was very late. The Lion, when he saw the Hare coming, bounded towards him. The Hare said--

"Uncle Lion, I know I am late, and you have cause to be angry. But really it is not my fault. There is another Lion in our part of the jungle, and he says that he is master, and you are nobody. In fact, when I showed him that I positively would come to you he was very angry."

"Ha!" said the Lion, roaring; "who says he is my master? Show him to me. I'll teach him who rules the forest."

"Come along then," said the Hare.

They went a long way, until they came to a well. The Hare looked down into the well. "He was here just now," said he.

The Lion looked in, and at the bottom he saw what looked like a Lion in the water. He shook his mane--the other Lion shook his mane. He roared--the echo of a roar came up from the bottom of the well. "Let me get at him!" roared the Lion. In he jumped--splash! Nothing more was ever heard of that Lion, and the beasts of the forest were glad to be left in peace. They put their heads together, and composed a verse of poetry, which is always sung in that forest on Sundays:--

> "The Hare is small, but by his wit
> He now has got the best of it;
> By folly down the Lion fell,
> And lost his life within the well."

# The Monkey's Bargains

Once upon a time an old Woman was cooking, and she ran short of fuel. She was so anxious to keep up her fire, that she tore out the hairs of her head, and threw them upon the flame instead of fuel.

A Monkey came capering by, and saw the old Woman at her fire.

"Old Woman," said the Monkey, "why are you burning your hair? Do you want to be bald?"

"O Monkey!" quoth the old Woman, "I have no fuel, and my fire will go out."

"Shall I get you some fuel, mother?" said the Monkey.
"That's like your kind heart," said the old Woman. "Do get me some fuel, and receive an old Woman's blessing."

The Monkey scampered away to the woods, and brought back a large bundle of sticks. The old Woman piled the dry sticks on the fire, and made a fine blaze. She put on her cooking-plank, and made four cakes.

All this while, the Monkey sat on his tail, and watched her. But when the cakes were done, and gave forth a delightful odour, the Monkey got up on his hind legs, and began dancing and cutting all manner of capers round about the cakes.

"O Monkey," said the old Woman, "why do you caper and dance around my cakes?"

"I gave you fuel," said the Monkey, "and won't you give me a cake?"

It seems to me that she might have thought of that without being asked; but she did not, so the Monkey had to ask for it.

Well, the old Woman gave the Monkey one cake, and the Monkey took his cake in high glee, and capered away.

On the way, he passed by the house of a Potter; and at the door of the Potter's house sat the Potter's son, crying his eyes out.

"What is the matter, little boy?" asked the Monkey.

"I am very hungry," whimpered the Potter's son, "and I have nothing to eat."

"Will a cake be of any use?" asked the kind Monkey.

The Potter's little Boy stretched out his hand, and into his hand the Monkey put his cake. Then the little Boy stopped crying, and ate the cake, but he forgot to say thank you. Perhaps he had never been taught manners, but the Monkey felt sad, because that was not the kind of thing he was used to.

The Potter's little Boy then went into the shop, and brought out four little earthenware pots, and began to play with them. He took no more notice of the Monkey, now that he had eaten his cake; but when the Monkey saw these earthenware pots, he began to dance and cut capers round them, like mad.

"Why are you dancing round my pots?" asked the little Boy. "Are you going to break them, Monkey?"

The Monkey replied, capering about all the while--

>"One old Woman, in a fix,
>Made me go and gather sticks;
>Then she gave me, for the sake
>Of the fuel, one sweet cake.
>That sweet cake to you I gave:
>In return, one pot I crave."

The Potter's little Boy was very much afraid of this dancing and singing Monkey, and perhaps he was a little bit ashamed of his ingratitude; so he gave the Monkey one of his four pots.

Away capered the Monkey, in high glee, carrying his pot. By-and-by he came to a place, where was a Cowherd's wife making curds in a mortar.

"What an odd thing to do, Mrs. Cowherd," said the Monkey. "Have you a fancy for making curds in a mortar?"

"No," said the Cowherd's wife, "but I have nothing better to make my curds in."

"Here's a pot which will do better than a mortar to make curds in," said the Monkey, offering the pot which he had received from the little Boy.

"Thank you, kind Mr. Monkey," said the Cowherd's wife. She took the pot and made curds in it. She took out the curds from the pot, and put them ready for eating, and some butter beside them. The Monkey watched her, sitting upon his tail.

Then the Monkey got up off his tail, and began to dance and cut capers round the curds and the butter.

"Why are you dancing about my butter?" said the Cowherd's wife. "Do you want to spoil it?"

Then the Monkey began to sing, as he capered about--

> "One old Woman, in a fix,
> Made me go and gather sticks;
> Then she gave me, for the sake
> Of the fuel, one sweet cake.
> Potter's son ate that, and he
> Gave a pot instead to me.
> Since to you I gave that pot,
> Give me butter, will you not?"

The wife of the Cowherd was much pleased with this song, as she was fond of music. "If your kindness," said she, "had not already earned the butter, your pretty song would be worth it." Then she gave him a good lump of butter.

Off went the Monkey in high glee, capering along with the lump of butter wrapped up in a leaf. As he went, he came to another place, where a Cowherd was grazing his kine. The Cowherd was sitting down at that moment, and enjoying his dinner, which consisted of a hunk of dry bread.

"Why do you eat dry bread, Mr. Cowherd?" asked the Monkey. "Are you fasting?"

"I am eating dry bread," quoth the Cowherd, "because I have nothing to eat with it."

"What do you say to this?" said the Monkey, cutting a caper, and offering to the Cowherd his lump of butter, wrapped up in a leaf.

"Ah," said the Cowherd, "prime." Not another word said he, but spread the butter upon his dry bread, and set to, with much relish.

The Monkey sat on his tail, and watched the Cowherd eating his meal. When the meal was eaten, up jumped the Monkey, and began capering and dancing, hopping and skipping, round and round the herd of kine.

"Ah," said the Bumpkin, "what are you a-doing that for?" The

Bumpkin was so ignorant that he thought the Monkey wanted to bewitch his cattle, and dry up all their milk.

The Monkey went on with his skips and capers, and as he capered, he sang this ditty:--

>"One old Woman, in a fix,
>Made me go and get her sticks;
>Then she gave me, for the sake
>Of the fuel, one sweet cake.
>Potter's son the sweet cake got,
>Gave me, in return, one pot.
>Cow-wife had the pot, and she
>Butter gave instead to me.
>This I gave to you just now:
>Will you give me, please, one cow?"

"Ah," said the Bumpkin, "'spose I must." He was afraid of the Monkey's spells, and so he gave him a cow.

Away capered the Monkey, in high glee, leading his cow by a string. "I am indeed getting on in the world," said he.

By-and-by, what should he see coming along the road, but the King himself. The King was fastened to the shafts of a cart, which he was slowly dragging along; and jogging by the side of this cart was an ox; and upon the ox sat the Queen. This King had very simple tastes, and so had the Queen.

"O King," said the Monkey, "why are you dragging your cart with your own royal hands?"

"This is the reason, O Monkey!" said the King. "My ox died in the forest, and I drag the cart because this cart will not drag itself."

"Come, sire," said the Monkey, "I don't like to see a King doing draught-work. Take this cow of mine, and welcome."

"Thank you, good and faithful Monkey," said the King. He mopped his brow, and yoked in the cow.

The Monkey began to dance and caper, jump and skip, round the Queen.

"What is the matter, worthy Monkey?" asked the King.

The Monkey began his ditty:--

> "One old Woman, in a fix,
> Made me go and gather sticks;
> Then she gave me, for the sake
> Of the fuel, one sweet cake.
> Potter's son the sweet cake got,
> Gave me in its place, one pot.
> Cow-wife had the pot, and she
> Butter gave instead to me.
> Bumpkin ate the butter, then
> Paid me with this cow again.
> Keep the cow, but don't be mean:
> All I ask for, is the Queen."

This seemed reasonable enough, so the King gave his Queen to the Monkey.

Away went the Monkey, capering along, and the Queen walked after (you see the King could not part with his ox as well as the Queen).

By-and-by they came to a Man sewing a button on to his shirt.

"Why, Man," said the Monkey, "why do you sew on your own buttons?"

"Because my wife is dead," said the Man.

"Here is a nice wife for you," said the Monkey. He gave the Queen to the Man. The Monkey then began his capers again, but all he could find to caper about, was a drum.

"You may have that drum, if you like," said the Man. "I only kept it because its voice reminded me of my wife, and now I have another."

"Thank you, thank you!" said the Monkey. "Now I am rich indeed!" Then he began to beat upon the drum, and sang:--

> "One old Woman, in a fix,
> Made me go and gather sticks;
> Then she gave me, for the sake
> Of the fuel, one sweet cake.
> Potter's son the sweet cake got,
> Gave me in its place, one pot.

Cow-wife had the pot, and she
Butter gave instead to me.
Bumpkin ate the butter, then
Gave a cow to me again.
King took cow, but was not mean,
For he paid me with a Queen.
Now I have a drum, that's worth
More than any drum on earth.
You are worth a queen, my drum!
Rub-a-dub-dub, dhum dhum dhum!"

So the Monkey capered away into the forest in
high glee, beating upon his drum, and he
has never been heard of since.

# The Monkey's Rebuke

In a certain village, whose name I know (but I think I will keep it to myself), in this village, I say, there was once a Milkman. I daresay you know that a Milkman is a man who sells milk; but I have seen milkmen who also sell water. That is to say, they put water in the milk which they sell, and so they get more money than they deserve. This was the sort of Milkman that my story tells of; and he was worse than the more part of such tricksters, since he actually filled his pans only half full of milk, and the other half all water. The people of that village were so simple and honest, that they never dreamt their Milkman was cheating them; and if the milk did seem thin, all they did was to shake their heads, and say, "What a lot of water the cows do drink this hot weather!"

By watering his milk, this Milkman got together a great deal of money: ten pounds it was, all in sixpences, because the villagers always bought sixpennyworth of milk a day.

When the Milkman had got ten pounds, that is to say, no less than four hundred silver sixpences, he thought he would go and try his tricks in another place, where there were more people to be cheated. So he put his four hundred silver sixpences in a bag, and set out.

After travelling a while, he came to a pond. He sat down by the pond to eat his breakfast, laying his bag of sixpences by his side; and after breakfast, he proceeded to wash his hands in the pond.

Now it so happened that this was the very pond where the Milkman came to water his milk. He came all this way out of the village, because he did not want to be seen by the people of the village. But there was one who saw him; and that was a Monkey, who lived in a tree which overhung the pond. Many a time and oft had this Monkey seen the Milkman pour water into the milk-cans, chuckling over the profit he was to make. This was a very worthy and well-educated Monkey, and he knew just as well as you or I know, that if you sell milk, you should put no water in it. When the Man stooped down to wash his hands in the pond, quietly, quietly down came the Monkey, swinging himself from branch to branch with his tail. Down he came to the ground, and picked up the bag of sixpences, and then up again to his perch in the tree.

The Monkey untied the mouth of the bag, and took out one sixpence, and, click! dropped it into the pond. The Milkman heard a tiny splash, but it did not trouble him, because he thought it was a nut or something that had fallen from the tree. Click! another sixpence. Click! went a third.

By this time the Milkman's hands were dry, and he looked round to pick up his bag, and get him gone. But no bag! Click! click! went the sixpences all this while; and now the Milkman began to look around him. Before long he espied the Monkey sitting on a branch with his beloved bag, and--O horror! dropping sixpences, click! click! click! one after another into the pond.

"I say, you Monkey!" shouted he, "that's my bag! What are you doing? bring me back my bag!"

"Not yet," said the Monkey, and went on dropping the sixpences, click! click! click!

The Milkman wept, the Milkman tore handfuls of hair out of his head; but the Monkey might have been made of stone for all the notice he took of the Milkman.

At last the Monkey had dropt two hundred sixpences into the pond. Then he tied up the mouth of the money-bag, and threw it down to the Milkman. "There, take your money," said the Monkey.

"And where's the rest of my money?" asked the Milkman, fuming with rage.

"You have all the money that is yours," said the Monkey. "Half of the money was the price of water from this pond, so to the pond I gave it."

The Milkman felt very much ashamed of himself, and went away, a sadder but a wiser man; and never again did he put water in his milk. And that is why I have not told you the name of the village where he lived; for now that he has turned over a new leaf, it would hardly be fair to rake up his old misdeeds against him.

# The Bull and the Bullfinch

Under a certain tree lived a wild Bull, and a Bullfinch had his nest in the branches. A Bull in a field is vicious enough, as I daresay you know; but a wild Bull is worse than anything. Wild Bulls are tremendously strong, and they can fight with almost any beast of the forest, even Lions and Tigers.

This wild Bull used to attack every creature that came near; and that, not for the sake of food, as Lions and Tigers do, but out of pure mischief. When the creature (were he man or beast) was killed, this wild Bull would leave the corpse lying, and begin to eat grass. But the little Bullfinch harmed nobody, unless it were a worm he would eat now and again for a treat. All day long he hopped about, picking up seeds, and singing away with all his throat. Many a time he saw the wild Bull gore some creature to death; and when he saw such things, tears would roll out of his eyes, because he could do nothing to help.

At last he thought to himself that he could at least warn the wild Bull of his wickedness, and clear his own conscience. So one morning, when the wild Bull was sitting under his tree, and looking around him, Bullfinch piped up, and said--

"Good brother Bull, I suppose we are akin somehow or other, because of our names."
"Yes, I daresay it may be so, Cousin Bullfinch," said the Bull.
"Well," says the Bullfinch, "allow me the right of a near kinsman to say something to you."
"All right, go ahead," said the Bull gruffly.
"Well," said the Bullfinch, clearing his throat (for he was a little frightened), "don't you know that murder is a very evil deed, and yet you do it every day of your life?"

"Impertinent speck!" said the Bull, getting up and walking away. He thought it cheeky that a bird so little should presume to rebuke a great big Bull. He did not remember, you see, that big bodies are often big fools, and precious goods are done up in small parcels. The warning of the little Finch was as the blowing of the wind; at least, so it seemed at the time, though afterwards (as you shall hear) the Bull did remember it.

So the Bull went on tossing and goring all that came within reach; and now he would have nothing to say to the poor little Bullfinch.

This went on, until one night a certain Lion had a dream. This Lion was King of the Forest, and he could conquer any creature who fought with him. In his dream the Lion thought that an angel stood before him, and said: "O Lion! in such a place, under a tree, lives a wild Bull, who does cruel murders every day upon innocent folk. By that tree is good pasture, and the wild Bull has grown very fat. I think he would make a nice meal for you; and at the same time you would be doing a good action in ridding the world of such a monster."

When day dawned, the Lion made no delay, but set out at once towards the place of the wild Bull. By-and-by he caught scent of the Bull, and then he uttered a terrible roar. The Bull heard the roar and was afraid; and still more feared he, when he saw this Lion approach, whom he knew to be the King of the Forest, and invincible.

"O Bull!" roared the Lion, "your hour has come. I am come to eat you, as a just punishment for your sins, and also because I am hungry."

At this the Bull trembled greatly, for he knew now that his sins had found him out. His knees gave way beneath him, and he was just about to sink to the ground, when the words of the Bullfinch came into his mind. Then he said--

"O mighty Lion! I have indeed deserved to be eaten, but I beg of you one last favour. Give me leave to bid farewell to a little kinsman of mine, Cousin Bullfinch, who lives in this tree, and at this moment is picking up seeds not far off."

The Lion was a good fellow, and had no wish to be hard on the Bull, so he said: "I give leave, O Bull, if you will promise on your honour to come back and be eaten."

The Bull gave his word that he would come back, and then went slowly away in search of the Bullfinch.

Master Bullfinch was at the moment eating his frugal breakfast of seeds. Suddenly he was aware that the wild Bull was approaching. He looked up, and seeing the dejected air of the Bull, he greeted him as cheerfully as he could, and then asked what the matter was? This Bullfinch bore no manner of grudge for the Bull's rudeness, because in his little body was a great heart, and he never thought of mean things.

"O Finchy, Finchy!" moaned the Bull, "look upon me for the last time! A hungry Lion has come to devour me, and it is of no use to resist; for he says that an angel has sent him to punish me for my sins."

"Poor old chap!" said the Bullfinch, "tell me all about it."

Then the wild Bull told him the dream which the Lion had seen.

"Ah," said the Bullfinch, "that is curious."
"Why?" asked the Bull.
"Because," said the Bullfinch, "I too had a dream last night, which I think the Lion ought to hear."

The wild Bull was not interested in the Bullfinch's dream; would you be interested in dreams, I wonder, if you expected to be eaten the next minute? However, he said nothing; and when Bullfinch fluttered his wings, and flew away towards the Lion, our friend the wild Bull followed slowly behind.

"Good morning, King Lion," said the little bird. "So you have had a dream?"
"Yes," said the Lion, and then he told the Bullfinch his dream.

"I had a dream too," said the Bullfinch, "and this it was. I dreamt that the same angel who came to you, came afterwards to me, and said, 'O Bullfinch! when the Lion comes to eat your friend the Bull, tell him that he was sent not to destroy, but to cure; and that now the Bull repents of his evil ways, the Lion may go back again to his forest.'"

"Oh, I am so glad!" said the Lion. "I am hungry, it is true, but I daresay I can find some other creature, who has committed no sins, and wants no curing. So good-bye, friend Bull, and don't do it again." So saying, the Lion shook hands with both of them, and went to look for a fawn.

Then the Bull, wild no longer, thanked his friend the Bullfinch for saving his life, and they became faster friends than ever. The Bull gored no more creatures, indeed he welcomed them as his guests; and in the fat pastures around that tree you might have seen, if you had been there, whole herds of deer and antelopes grazing without any fear; and the Bull lived in their midst to a green old age, till he died respected and went to a happier world.